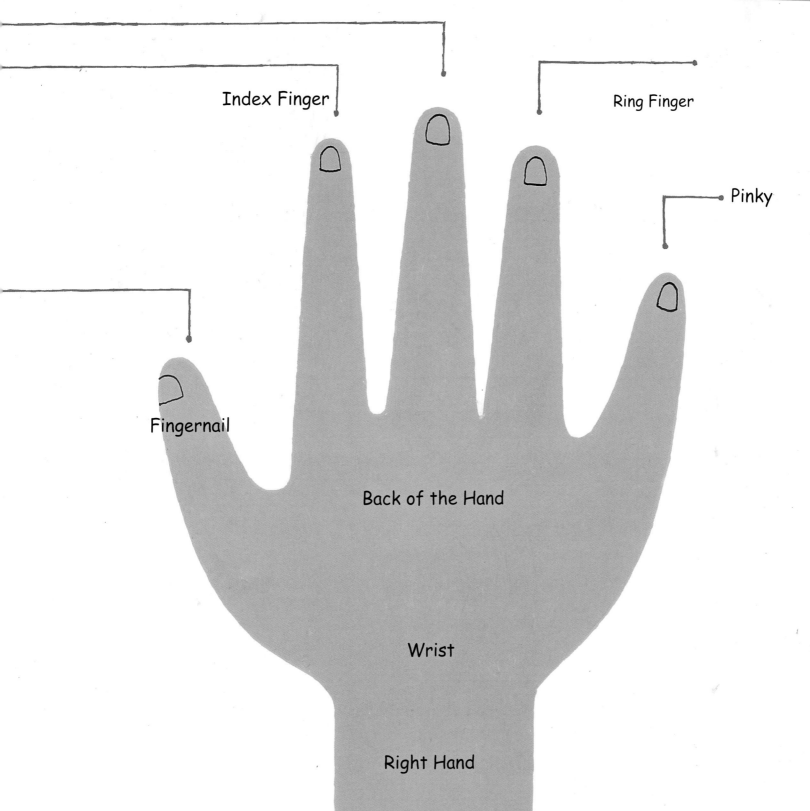

Index Finger

Ring Finger

Pinky

Fingernail

Back of the Hand

Wrist

Right Hand

About the Author
Sung Eun Kim majored in Education at Ewha Women's. Her books include *Magpie and Soh Dahm's Puzzle Play, Troublemaker TtoTto, The Monster That Lives at the Dentist Office, Let's Play in the Sand, and Floating Little Boat*, among others.

About the Illustrator
Ji Won Lee studied illustration, and has been illustrating books for children since college. Her first illustrated book was *What Is at the Edge of the Sky?*, and her other books include *Go! Save the Green Team's Whale, Gershwin, Huh Seng's Story, Rainbow Poop, Bba Bba Ra Ghee*.

Tantan Publishing Knowledge Storybook ***The Hand Manual***

www.TantanPublishing.com

Published in the U.S. in 2016 by TANTAN PUBLISHING, INC.
4005 w Olympic Blvd., Los Angeles, CA 90019-3258

©Copyright 2016 by Dong-hwi Kim
English Edition

ISBN: 978-1-939248-15-2

Printed in Korea

The Hand Manual

Written by Sung Eun Kim   Illustrated by Ji Won Lee

TanTan Publishing

SPREAD your fingers apart!

Make a CIRCLE with your fingers!

SQUEEZE your fingers together!

RAISE your thumb!

Make a FIST!

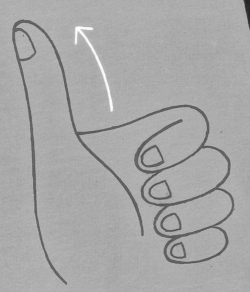

POINT your index finger!

Are both your hands moving correctly? Then let's go and learn how to use them one by one!

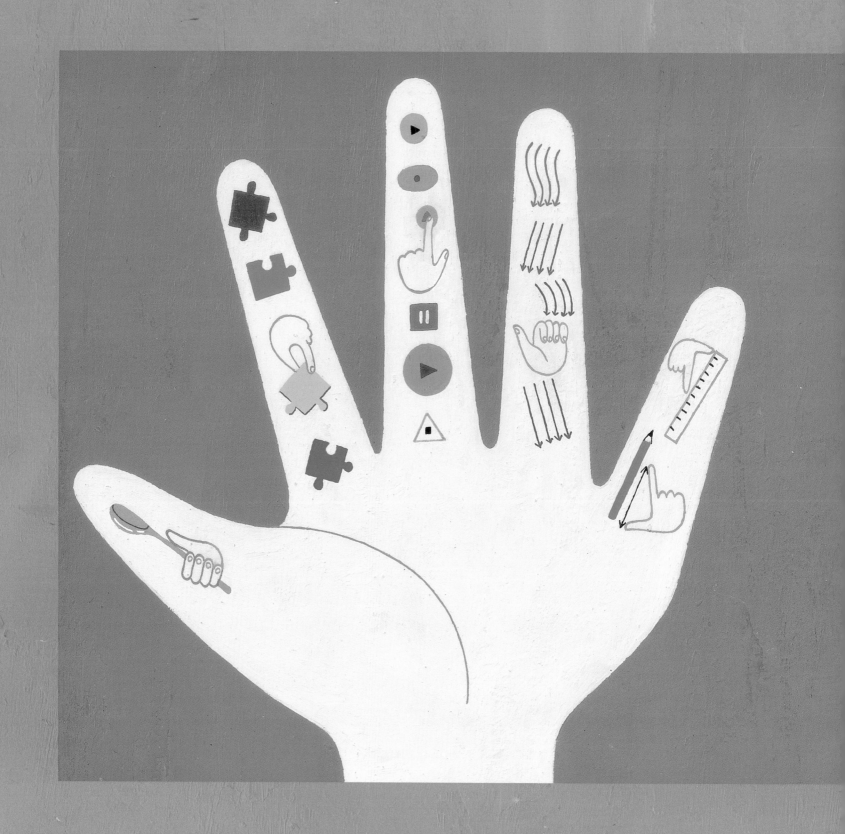

Working Hands, Busy Hands

 Everyday Uses

 Grabbing

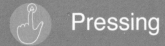 Pressing

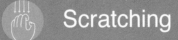 Scratching

 Measuring

✕ Everyday Uses

We use our hands for many things every day, such as to eat, dress, and wash.

Make your teeth squeaky-clean with a toothbrush.

Brush your hair neatly with a comb.

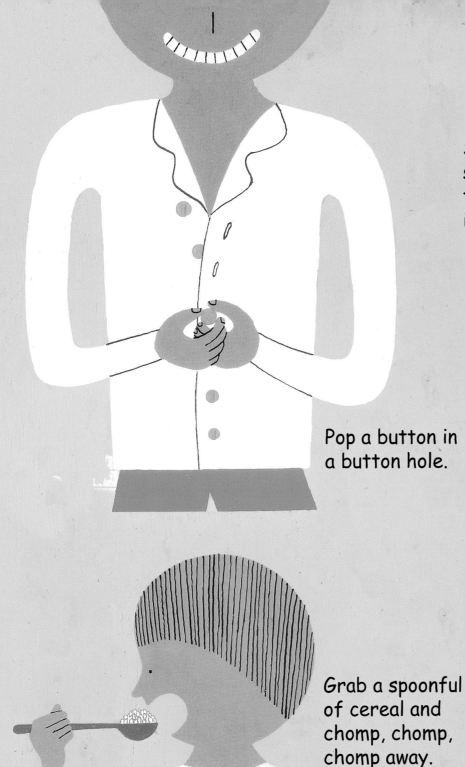

Slide your shoelace through the holes and tie it in a tight bow.

Pop a button in a button hole.

Grab a spoonful of cereal and chomp, chomp, chomp away.

Right Hand, Left Hand

You have two hands, your right hand and your left hand, with five fingers on each hand. Each of the five fingers have different names and lengths, but if you use them all together you can accomplish many things. Someone who uses their right hand most of the time is right-handed, and someone who uses their left hand most of the time is left-handed.

✖ Grabbing

If you press your thumb and one of the other fingers together, you can easily grab or pick things up.

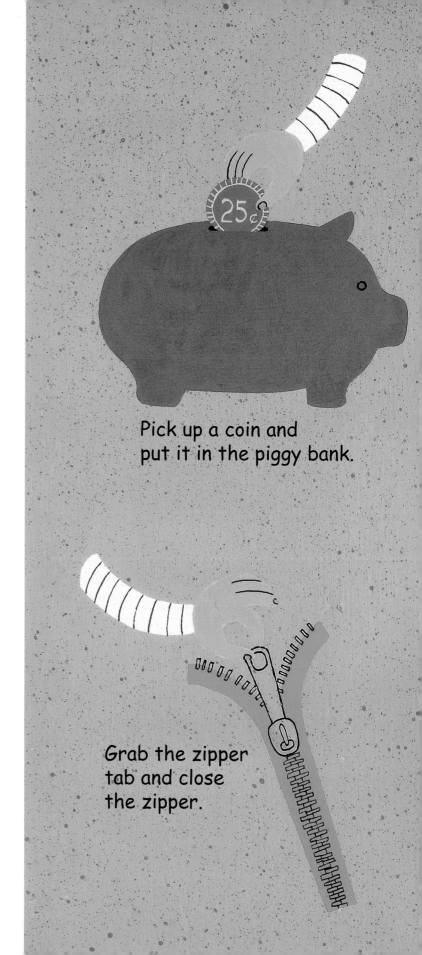

Pick up a coin and put it in the piggy bank.

Grab the zipper tab and close the zipper.

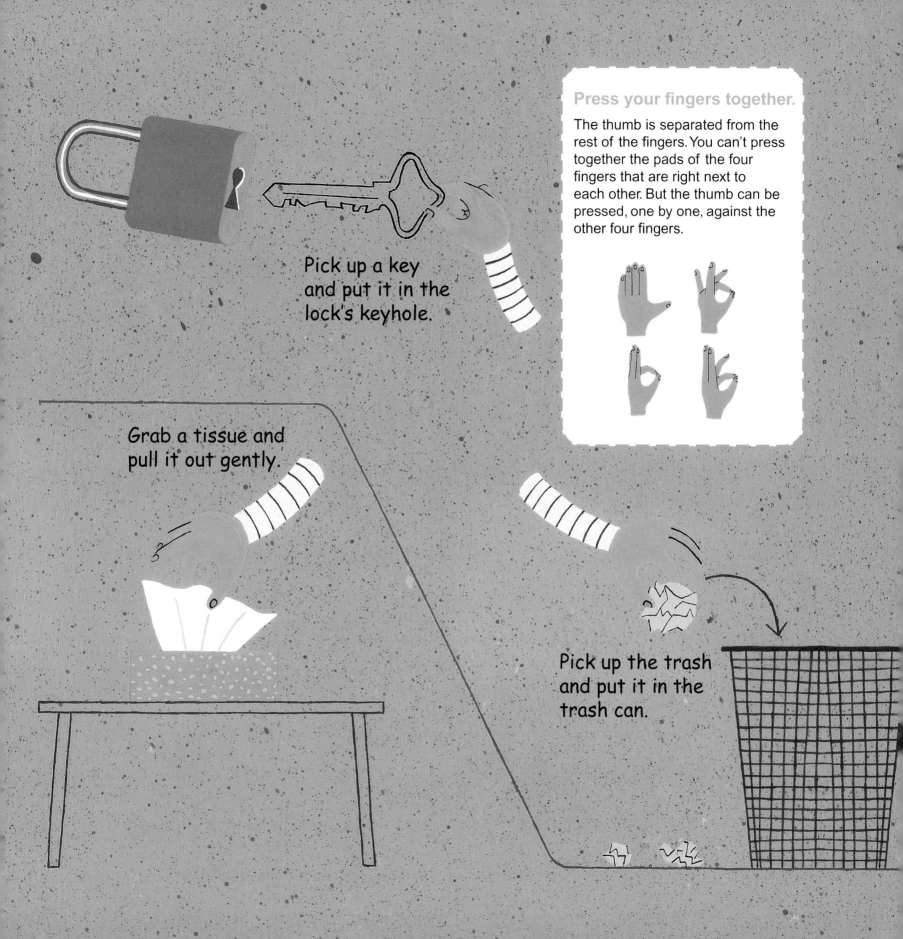

Pick up a key and put it in the lock's keyhole.

Press your fingers together.

The thumb is separated from the rest of the fingers. You can't press together the pads of the four fingers that are right next to each other. But the thumb can be pressed, one by one, against the other four fingers.

Grab a tissue and pull it out gently.

Pick up the trash and put it in the trash can.

⋇ Pressing

Press buttons firmly with your fingers, and you can control all sorts of machines.

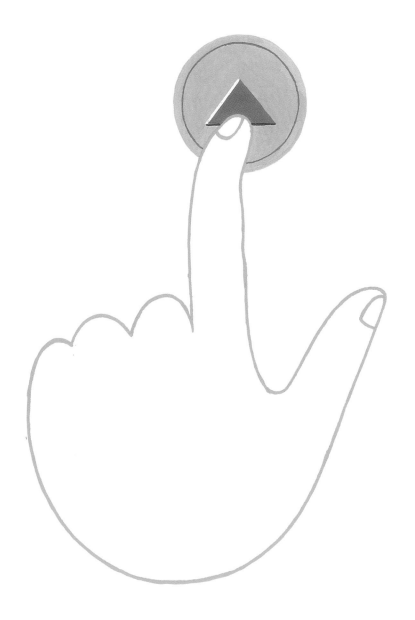

Press the light switch to turn the light on and off.

To make a phone call, press the numbers.

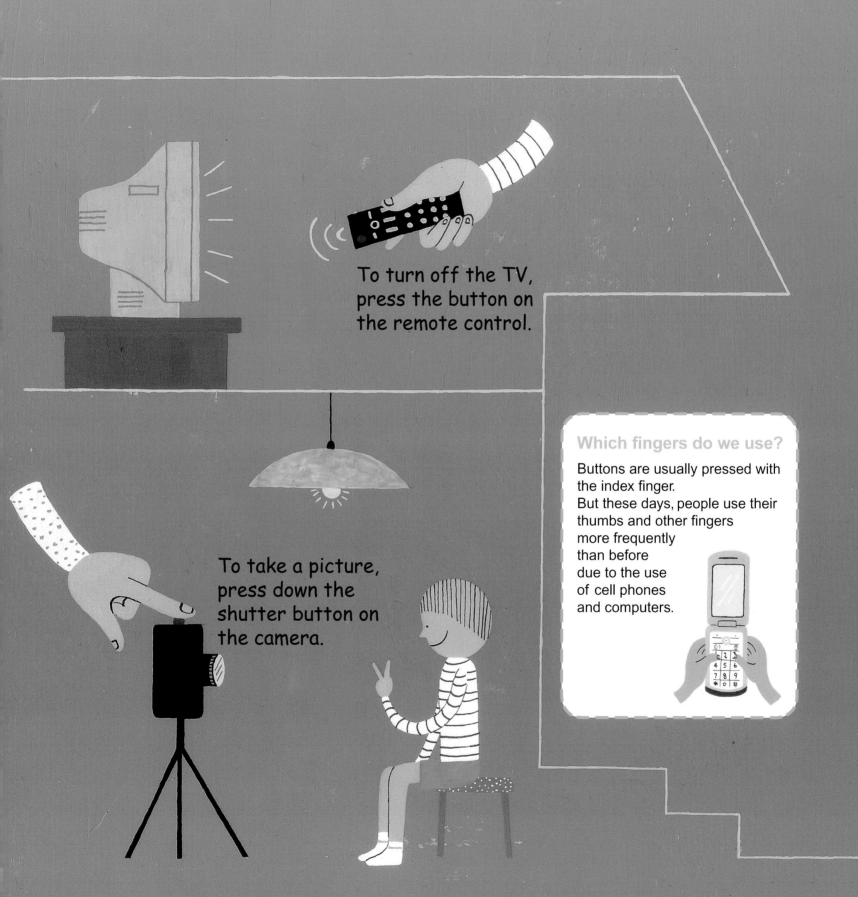

To turn off the TV, press the button on the remote control.

To take a picture, press down the shutter button on the camera.

Which fingers do we use?

Buttons are usually pressed with the index finger.
But these days, people use their thumbs and other fingers more frequently than before due to the use of cell phones and computers.

✳ Scratching

At the end of your fingers are hard fingernails.
When you have an itch, you can use your fingers for relief.

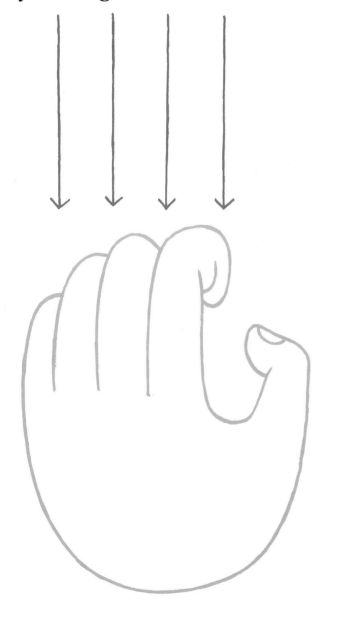

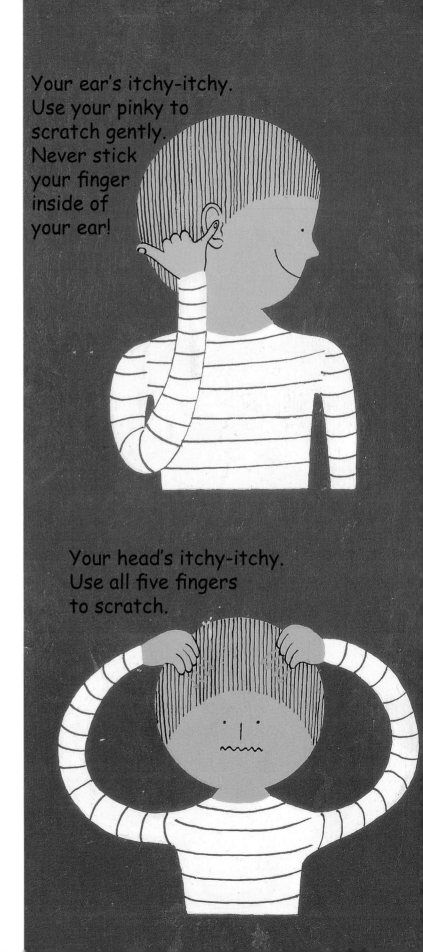

Your ear's itchy-itchy. Use your pinky to scratch gently. Never stick your finger inside of your ear!

Your head's itchy-itchy. Use all five fingers to scratch.

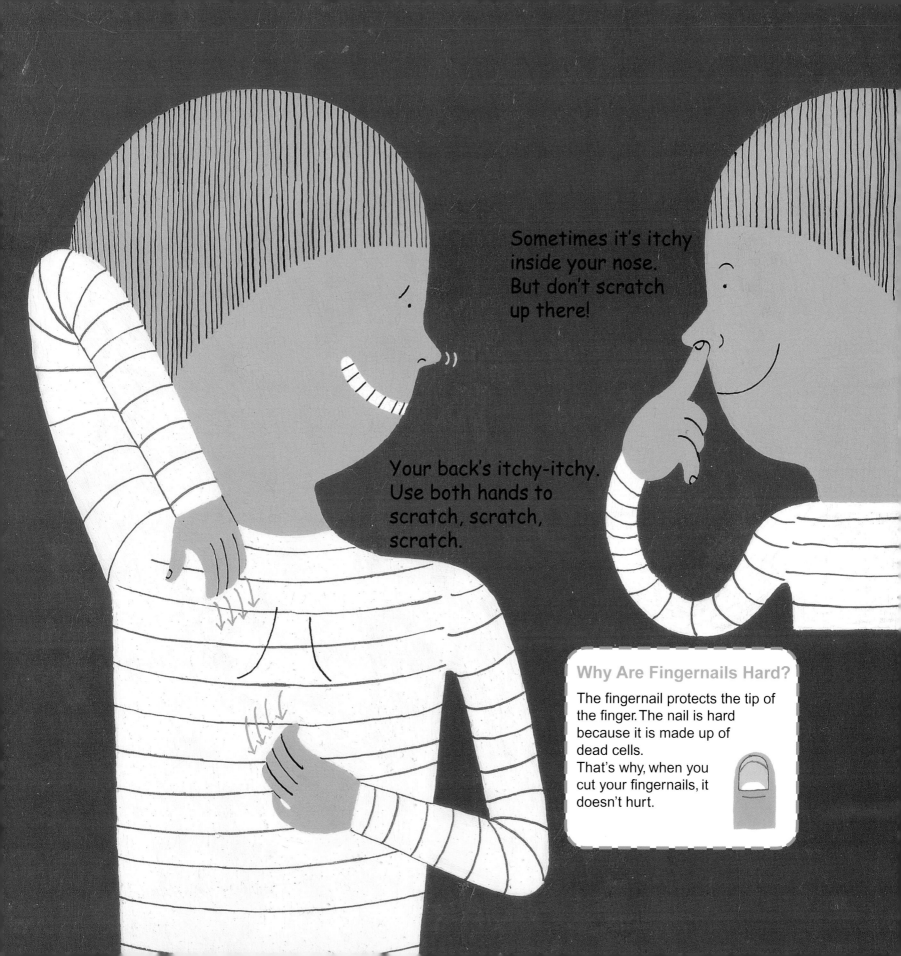

Sometimes it's itchy
inside your nose.
But don't scratch
up there!

Your back's itchy-itchy.
Use both hands to
scratch, scratch,
scratch.

Why Are Fingernails Hard?

The fingernail protects the tip of
the finger. The nail is hard
because it is made up of
dead cells.
That's why, when you
cut your fingernails, it
doesn't hurt.

✳ Measuring

You can use your fingers to measure length, And you can use your hands to measure temperature and weight.

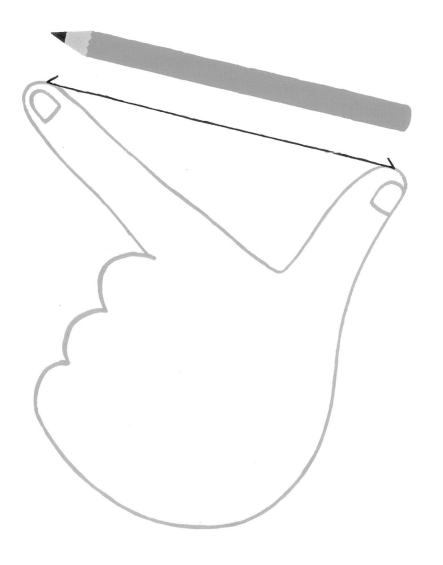

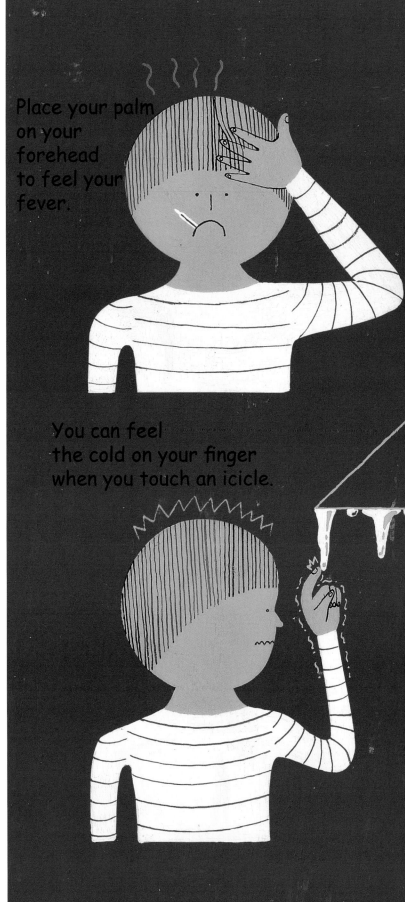

Place your palm on your forehead to feel your fever.

You can feel the cold on your finger when you touch an icicle.

You can compare the weight of objects when you hold them in your hands.

Feel With Your Hands!

There are lots of small nerves at the ends of your fingertips. That's why, when you touch something with your hands, you can easily tell if it's soft, prickly, hard, bumpy, hot, or cold without even looking at it.

eraser

When you spread your thumb and another finger, that length is a "span."

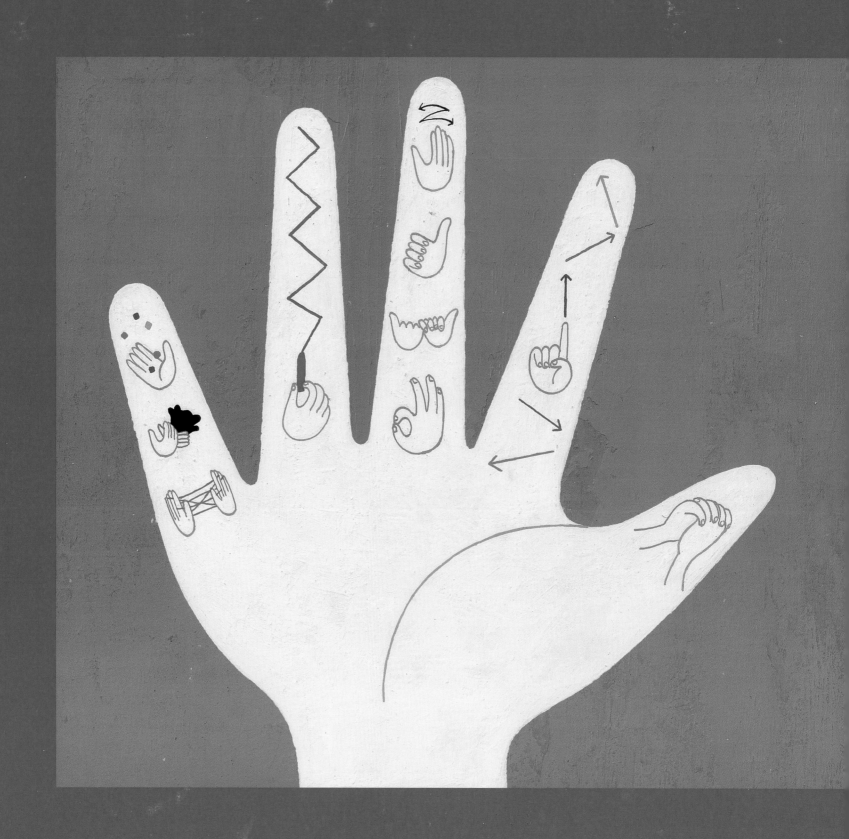

Happy Hands, Expressive Hands

 Playing

 Creating

 Speaking

 Communicating

 Sharing Emotions

Playing

Even without toys you can have fun playing just with your hands.

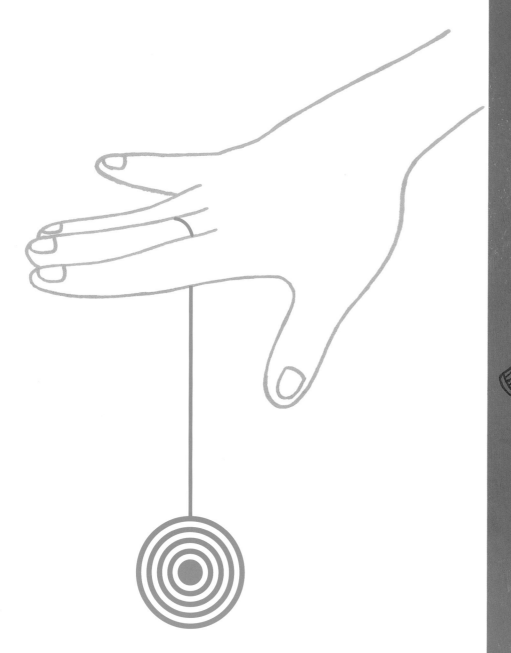

Illuminate your hands with a flashlight and make hand shadow puppets.

Remember!

Each person's body is their own private space. Remember to keep your hands to yourself.

Spread yarn between your fingers and play cat's cradle.

Take a friend by the hand and raise your thumbs so you can thumb wrestle.

Draw something on your hand and make a hand puppet.

✗ Creating

You can use your hands to make pretty drawings and play lovely music, too.

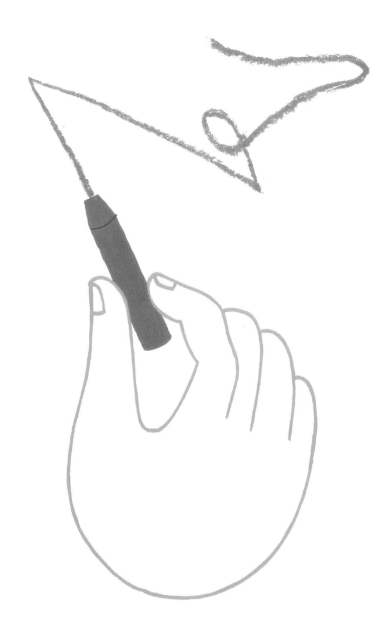

Grab a paintbrush and paint a picture.

Mold clay to create a new shape.

Play an instrument and make beautiful sounds.

Take the conducting baton and lead the musical performance.

Try this!
You can show your appreciation and encouragement by clapping.

✖ Speaking

Even when you don't speak with your mouth, you can still communicate with your hands.

OK

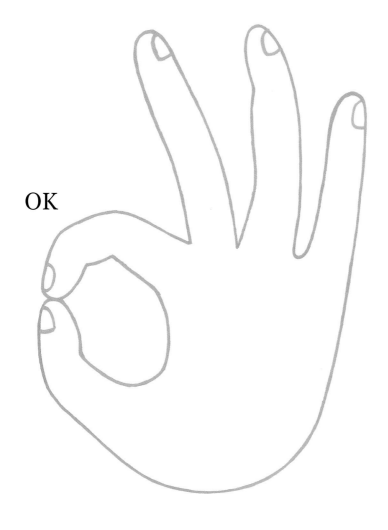

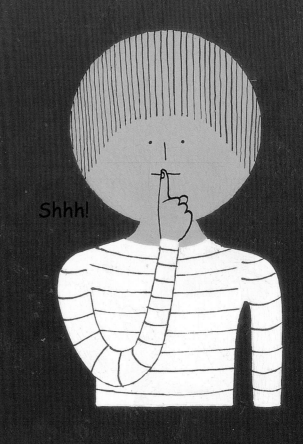

Shhh!

Remember!

Hands can hurt people, too. Remember to be gentle.

✳ Communicating

You can use your hand like
an arrow.
Use your index finger to
give directions.
Show numbers by displaying
as many fingers as you'd like.

Please sit here.

Elderly Section

Remember!
Pointing at someone can hurt their feelings.
Remember to be kind.

ICE CREAM

Three, please.

✖ Sharing Emotions

When you really want something, whether you're happy or sad or scared or embarrassed, you can express emotions with your hands.

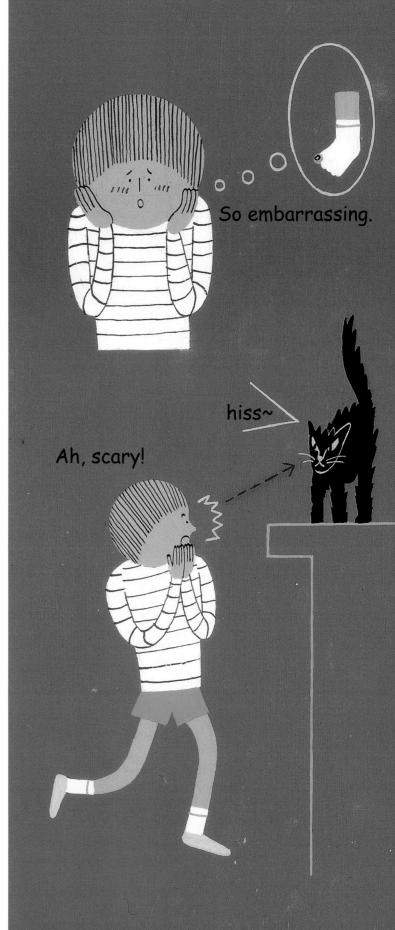

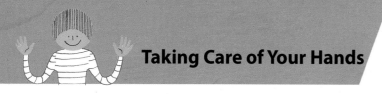

Wash your hands thoroughly and regularly.

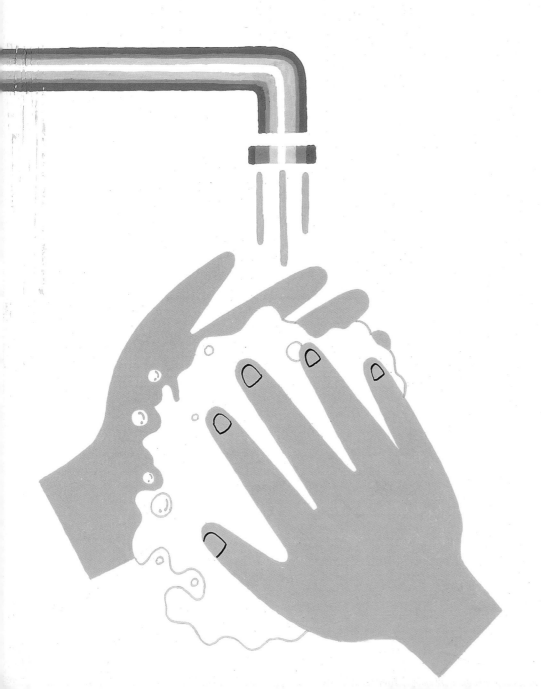

Rub your palms first.

The back of your hands, too.

Don't forget to clean in between your fingers

And under your fingernails.

Clip your fingernails neatly and evenly.

Don't leave them too long. Clip them often!

When it's cold, wear gloves or mittens.

Gloves and mittens keep your hands from freezing!

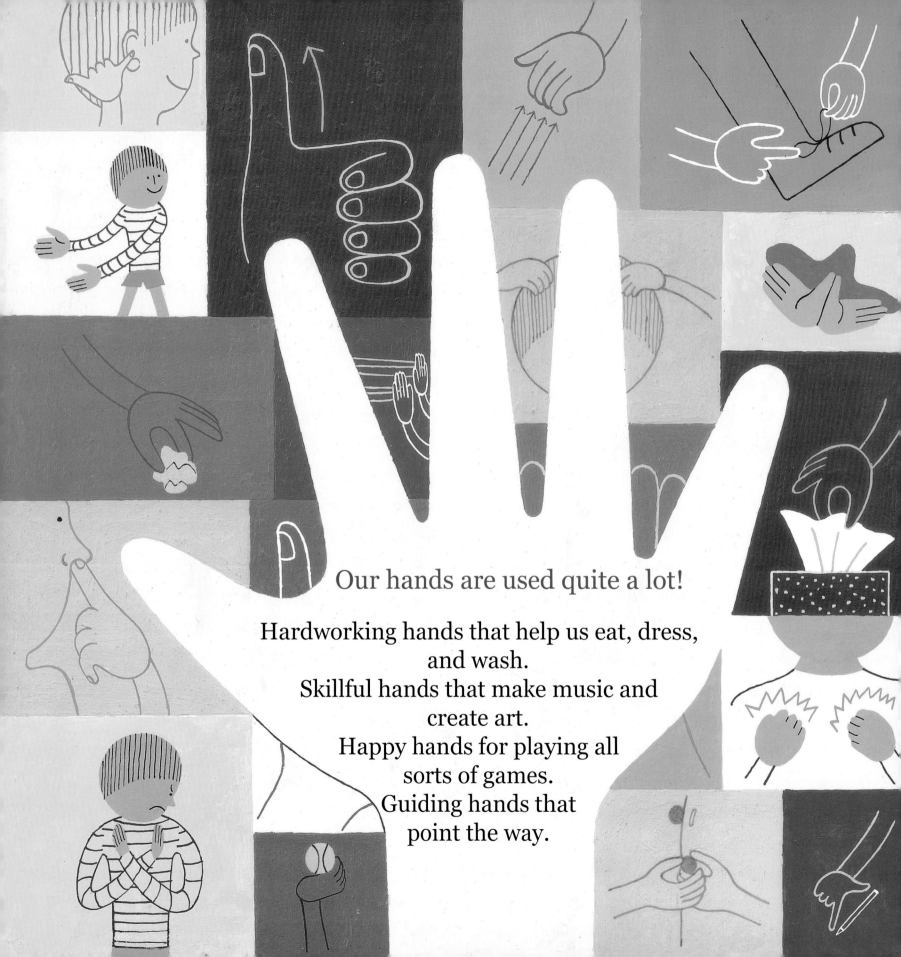

Our hands are used quite a lot!

Hardworking hands that help us eat, dress, and wash.
Skillful hands that make music and create art.
Happy hands for playing all sorts of games.
Guiding hands that point the way.

But the best hands
give a loving squeeze
and hold us close.

Hand Certificate

Name: _____

Birthdate: _____

Certified by: _____

Your hands are the greatest hands!

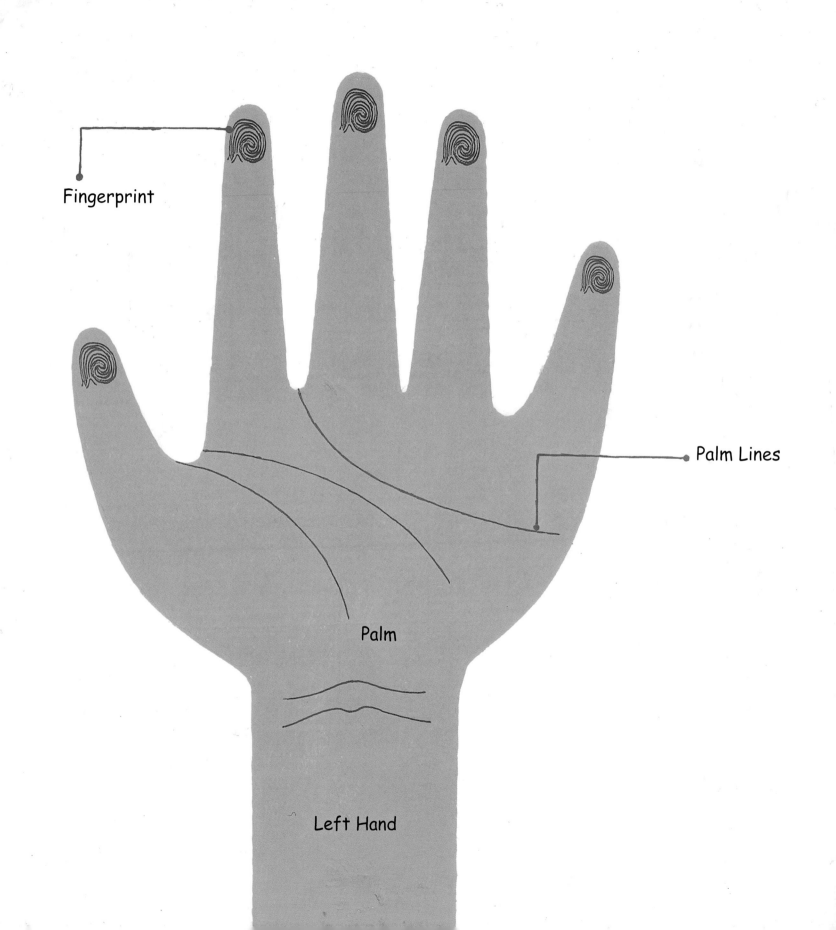

Fingerprint

Palm Lines

Palm

Left Hand